Bound for Snow

by Alison Hart

illustrated by Arcana Studios

★ American Girl®

Published by American Girl Publishing
Copyright © 2012 American Girl

Questions or comments? Call 1-800-845-0005,
visit americangirl.com, or write to Customer Service,
American Girl, 8400 Fairway Place, Middleton, WI 53562-0497.

Printed in China
12 13 14 15 16 17 18 19 LEO 10 9 8 7 6 5 4 3 2 1

All American Girl and Innerstar University marks and Amber™, Emmy™,
Isabel™, Logan™, Neely™, Paige™, Riley™, and Shelby™ are trademarks
of American Girl.

Illustrated by Thu Thai at Arcana Studios

Special thanks to Mary, Emma, and Greta Thiel at Wolfsong Adventures
in Mushing, Bayfield, Wisconsin; and to Kris Kruse-Elliott, D.V.M, Ph.D.,
a Professional Ski Instructors of America Level 3 instructor and retired Central
Division examiner, and a Primary Movements Teaching System trainer and
coach in Redwood City, California.

Welcome to Innerstar University! At this imaginary, one-of-a-kind school, you can live with your friends in a dorm called Brightstar House and find lots of fun ways to let your true talents shine. Your friends at Innerstar U will help you find your way through some challenging situations, too.

When you reach a page in this book that asks you to make a decision, choose carefully. The decisions you make will lead to more than 20 different endings! (*Hint:* Use a pencil to check off your choices. That way, you'll never read the same story twice.)

Want to try another ending? Read the book again—and then again. Find out what would have happened if you'd made *different* choices. Then head to www.innerstarU.com for even more book endings, games, and fun with friends.

Innerstar Guides

Every girl needs a few good friends to help her find her way. These are the friends who are always there for **you**.

Emmy

A brave girl who loves swimming and boating

Isabel

A confident girl with a funky sense of style

Riley

A good sport, on the field and off

Paige

A nature lover who leads hikes and campus cleanups

Amber

An animal lover and
a loyal friend

Neely

A creative girl who loves
dance, music, and art

Logan

A super-smart girl
who is curious about
EVERYTHING

Shelby

A kind girl who is there
for her friends—and loves
making NEW friends!

Innerstar U Campus

1. Rising Star Stables
2. Star Student Center
3. Brightstar House
4. Starlight Library
5. Sparkle Studios
6. Blue Sky Nature Center

7. Real Spirit Center
8. Five-Points Plaza
9. Starfire Lake & Boathouse
10. U-Shine Hall

11. Good Sports Center
12. Shopping Square
13. The Market
14. Morningstar Meadow

ou're sprawled out on a sofa, doing nothing in the attic of Brightstar House. All around you, your friends are busy. Amber is reading a book on dog-sledding. Becca is playing a snowboarding video game, and Paige is stretching on a yoga mat. The most exciting thing you can do is yawn. You've been such a couch potato lately. You definitely need a change, before you sprout roots.

"Are you going to Sky-High Mountain Resort for the Snow Sports weekend?" Paige asks Becca.

Becca keeps playing as she answers, "You bet! The slopes have four feet of snow. Should be awesome."

You perk up. You like to ski—at least you did last year. Your skis and poles should be in your dorm closet somewhere. Maybe you'll look for them tomorrow, you decide with another yawn.

Turn to page 10.

"Woo-hoo!" Becca cheers as she finishes the game. Her face is flushed with excitement. "Snowboarding is my new favorite sport. I'm pumped that Innerstar U organized a weekend at the resort. I can't *wait* to hit the snowboarding park. Are the rest of you going? The van leaves Friday afternoon."

Paige nods. "I'm going cross-country skiing," she says. "And I hear we get to stay at a chalet overnight. How about you two?" she asks, looking at you and Amber.

"Umm . . ." You hesitate. You don't want to admit that you were too lazy to even read the sign-up sheet.

"You should come!" Becca urges. "You'd love snowboarding."

Snowboarding *would* be something new, and Becca sure is having fun with her video game. A Snow Sports weekend sounds almost daring. Are you ready to get up off the couch and try it?

Turn to page 12.

Just then Amber pipes up. "I'm going to the mountains, too, but not for snowboarding or skiing," she says. "I'm taking *mushing* lessons—you know, dogsledding—at Sky-High Dog School."

"Wow, that sounds cool!" you say. "I love dogs."

"Cool, but a lot of *work*," Becca adds. "I'd rather zoom down a snowy mountain."

"I'm training Pepper for the Thompsons," Amber explains. "Huskies are naturals at pulling sleds. It's helped Pepper get out some of his energy, and he loves it."

Sounds like fun, you think. And like snowboarding, it's definitely something you've never tried before.

"On Saturday a group is going to the dogsledding school for a lesson," Amber says. "My friend Jen helps teach a class. You should come." She's looking at you.

"I think you'd like snowboarding better," Becca says, looking at you, too.

You're torn. A moment ago you were bored to tears, and now you have two exciting offers. Which will you choose?

If you pick dogsledding, turn to page 14.

If you pick snowboarding, turn to page 16.

Amber suggests that before you head up the mountain to try dogsledding with Honey, you should practice a few basic commands with her on campus. You meet outside Pet-Palooza in a grassy, fenced-in play area.

Amber hands you a leash, and you hook it to Honey's collar. Immediately she leaps forward, and you have to run to keep up. You try to slow her down, but she doesn't respond. So much for her previous training!

When you finally get Honey under control, you ask Amber, "Are you sure Honey will like dogsledding?"

Amber shrugs. "Pepper loves sledding so far," she says, "but he's a husky, and pulling sleds comes naturally to him. Retrievers were bred for hunting. Honey sure likes to pull, and"—she laughs as Honey gives another tug on her leash, pulling you off balance—"she certainly has lots of energy."

You're not laughing. Teaching this energetic dog to pull a sled is starting to sound less like fun and more like *work*.

 If you decide to brave that first lesson with Honey anyway, turn to page 20.

If you decide that Honey needs to get out some of her energy first, turn to page 17.

Thursday after school, you meet Amber at Pet-Palooza, a day-care center for animals. You find Amber in the play area with Honey, a bouncy retriever with golden, silky fur. Amber introduces you to Honey's owners, Mr. and Mrs. Rojas, and their son, Russ.

As you step into the play area, Honey bounds over and nearly knocks you off your feet. You squat down, and she washes your face with kisses. Amber gently scolds Honey and makes her sit.

"I apologize for Honey," Mr. Rojas says. "Dog training has helped, but she's still a handful. She's too much for Russ because she has so much energy."

"Have you given any more thought to dogsledding school?" Amber asks him. "Lots of energy is a must for the sport. Honey would love it, I think, and I'll bet we could find *someone* here on campus who could train her." Amber grins at you.

Mrs. Rojas looks your way, too, her eyes lighting up. "Oh, are you interested?" she asks.

You glance at Honey, who now has a ball in her mouth and is whining, begging for someone to throw it. The young dog *is* a handful, but she's sweet, so you don't have to think twice before telling Amber and Mr. and Mrs. Rojas, "I'd love to work with Honey."

 Turn to page 13.

"I'd like to try dogsledding someday," you tell Amber and Becca, "but I think I'll start with snowboarding lessons this weekend."

"Great!" Becca says, slapping palms with you. "You can rent a snowboard at the resort. Boots and a helmet, too. But don't worry about lessons—I'll teach you everything you need to know. Like ollies and aerial one-eighties." She turns back to her video game. "Watch this . . ."

You study the boarders zipping down a snowy hill on the TV screen. These moves look totally different from the ones you learned skiing. But soon, you're playing the game beside Becca, doing virtual tricks in a halfpipe and imagining yourself hitting the slopes. The weekend at Sky-High Mountain Resort is going to be so much fun!

Turn to page 18.

At Pet-Palooza the next day, you ask permission to take Honey for a jog down the paths around campus. Your goal is to get her to burn up some of her energy so that she'll listen better during the training sessions.

Happily, Honey trots beside you. You pass ducks on the lake and girls throwing Frisbees. Honey pricks her ears at them but keeps jogging along beside you. *This is working,* you think, except that the exercise is wearing you out.

"Hi!" someone hollers from behind you. You turn around and see Isabel and Riley in-line skating toward you. They roll to a stop.

"Hi, Honey," says Riley, stooping to greet the retriever, who leaps up to give her kisses.

"Down, Honey," you command, but of course she doesn't listen.

"Sorry, Riley," you say after you finally get Honey to sit—for a second. "I'm hoping to train Honey for dog-sledding, but she's so full of energy that she won't even listen to my commands."

🐾 Turn to page 29.

Friday after classes you pack an overnight bag and meet Becca at the school van. Your friend Emmy is there, too, holding her snowboard. The two are talking excitedly about snowboarding. "Last weekend I rode a rail," Becca says.

"You'll have to teach me!" Emmy tells her. "I've only done a tabletop."

You feel kind of left out—and definitely confused. "I won't be doing any rails yet," you admit, trying to sound as if you know what a rail is.

"Don't worry, you'll get the hang of it," Emmy assures you.

The van quickly fills up with girls. Paige gets on with cross-country skis. Your friend Shelby is there, too, with skate skis. "I'm trying them out this weekend," she says.

"I tried skate skis last year," Becca says. "But I like snowboarding better because of all the tricks I can do."

"I like cross-country skiing the best," Paige chimes in.

As the van winds its way up the mountain, the girls playfully argue about the different snow sports. Halfway to the top, you pass Sky-High Dog School. Dogsledding sounds like fun, but you're glad you took the snowboarding challenge for this weekend.

 Turn to page 30.

On Saturday, you and Honey head to Sky-High Dog School with Amber and Pepper. You meet Jen, Amber's friend and the assistant instructor. The group begins the lesson by working on the basics: sit, down, stay, and come.

"You don't want your dog to heel," Jen tells the group, "because your dog needs to stay in front of the sled and not by your side. But your dog *does* need to listen."

Uh-oh. Listening isn't exactly one of Honey's strengths.

Because Amber and Pepper have taken a few lessons, they're soon working with the lead instructor on pulling a practice sled. By the end of the lesson, you and Honey are the only ones still working with Jen. Every time Honey sees a squirrel or bird, her hunting instinct kicks in and she drags you through the snow. Even the dog biscuits Jen uses to reward good behavior don't work.

"I give up," you tell Amber as you leave class.

"It's too early to give up," she says with an encouraging smile. "Honey gets pretty distracted, I know," she says. "Maybe she needs extra training on her own, away from the other dogs. Or maybe you need tastier treats." She holds up one of the biscuits from class and wrinkles her nose.

 If you take Honey to a quiet place to work on the basics, turn to page 22.

 If you try special treats to get Honey to pay attention, turn to page 23.

On Sunday, for your second lesson, you take Honey to a quiet area behind the dog school. She's away from the other dogs, and you're hoping that the privacy fence will keep out the *squirrels*, too.

With fewer distractions, Honey's attention is all on you. Soon she's performing the basic commands. She *does* remember her previous dog training, you realize. The trick was getting her to focus on you and really listen.

Amber comes to watch. "Great job!" she says, clapping, after you make Honey sit and stay. "That's the best Honey has obeyed since she came to Pet-Palooza. I think she's ready for the next step."

Amber holds up a harness, and you grin excitedly. You give Honey the stay command while Amber shows you how to put on the harness. Honey quivers with energy, but she stays in one place long enough for you and Amber to get the harness strapped on correctly.

"Good girl!" you praise. When Honey twirls around, she doesn't seem to mind the harness at all.

This just might work!

Turn to page 24.

"What kind of treats should I try?" you ask Amber. She spends a lot of time at Pet-Palooza and is a pro at these things.

Amber doesn't hesitate. "Cheese," she says. "Honey is all about cheese treats. We have some at Pet-Palooza. Let's pick some up when the van drops us off today."

The following afternoon, you discover that Amber's right: Honey is a total cheese lover. As soon as you hold up a cheesy treat, her attention is on you—well, not on *you* exactly, but on the treat in your hand, which is still an improvement over yesterday.

With the new treats as her reward, Honey shows how smart she is by following all the basic commands. She sits, she stays, and she comes when you call her. You're so proud that you demonstrate the tricks again in front of the other volunteers at Pet-Palooza. They clap, and Honey prances happily, her silky tail waving.

When the Rojas family comes to pick up Honey, you show Russ how to give the sit command and then reward Honey with a treat. The whole family cheers, and Honey barks as if she knows just how well she has done.

You puff up your chest a little, too, and think how easy training Honey was today—now that you've found the right treat. Teaching Honey how to pull a sled will be a piece of . . . cheese.

 Turn to page 25.

You thought Honey had made real progress, but the next Saturday at dog school, it's as if she's forgotten everything she learned. She doesn't listen, and when she's close to the other dogs in class, she barks and wants to play.

When you try to put on the harness, Honey thinks you're playing tug-of-war. Yanking the harness from your grip, she shakes it with her teeth.

"Honey!" you holler in frustration. "Bad girl!" She cowers, and instantly you feel terrible. Amber and Jen hear you yelling and come over to see what's going on.

"Sorry," you apologize. "I shouldn't have yelled. I'm just worried that Honey will never get the hang of this. As soon as she gets around other dogs, she's out of control."

"Don't give up yet," Amber says quickly. "Pepper is experienced enough that he might be able to teach Honey if the two of them are teamed together."

"And remember, too, that not all dogs are suited for sledding," Jen adds. "Honey might do better at something like *skijoring*—a sport where a person on skis is pulled by just one or two dogs."

You blow out a sigh of relief. "Thanks, guys," you say. "I definitely need to try something new with Honey."

What will you try?

 If you decide to try skijoring, turn to page 28.

 If you think Pepper can help Honey learn to dogsled, turn to page 26.

You're feeling confident when you head to Sky-High for the next training session. In your coat pocket, you've stashed your baggie of cheese treats.

This time, when you and Honey go through the basic commands, the pup responds perfectly. The other students stop what they're doing to clap, and Honey struts as if onstage.

Later, Jen shows you how to put the harness on Honey. Then she takes it off and lets you try it yourself. You slip on the harness and adjust it without a hitch. "Ta-da!" you say proudly. "Next step—pulling a sled!"

Standing back, you smile at Honey. But she tucks her tail and gives you a mournful look.

"What's going on?" you ask Jen.

"This is only the first time you've tried the harness on Honey," Jen says. "Try again tomorrow at Pet-Palooza, where she's comfortable, and see how she reacts."

 Turn to page 27.

Amber is excited to hear that you're not ready to give up on dogsledding. "Let's try working Honey and Pepper together after today's lesson," she says.

"If we even get *through* the lesson," you joke as Honey drags you toward a chipmunk.

You do get through the next half hour, but as Honey ignores command after command, you start to wonder if maybe Honey isn't the problem. Maybe it's *you*. You've never trained a sled dog before. How can you teach Honey when you're still learning yourself?

When you meet up with Amber after class, she's bursting with enthusiasm. "I *know* that Pepper will be able to help train Honey," she says. "I can feel it."

"I'm glad somebody's feeling confident," you say. "I wish I were, too. Maybe Pepper can help train *me*," you joke.

Only it's not a joke, you realize. Maybe working with a more experienced dog *would* boost your skills.

 If you try to work with Pepper to build your own skills, turn to page 38.

 If you stick with training Honey alongside Pepper, turn to page 35.

The next day after history class, Amber goes with you to Pet-Palooza. She and Pepper are ahead of you in dog-sledding training, so you're glad for her help.

When you put the harness on Honey, she does a repeat performance—lying down with a pitiful doggie groan.

"Boy, she sure doesn't like the harness," Amber says as the two of you stare down at Honey.

You let out a sigh. "Jen warned me that not all dogs take to the harness—or to the sport," you say.

"Maybe you need to find out what Honey *does* like to do," Amber suggests.

"Good advice, except she can't talk," you say grumpily.

"Sure she can," Amber counters. "She just doesn't use words." Amber points to the retriever, whose head is buried between her paws. "Right now, she's telling you *exactly* how she feels."

Amber's right. Honey has been telling you all along that she doesn't like the harness. But what *does* she like? Cheese treats, definitely. And retrieving tennis balls. And doing tricks in front of the volunteers at Pet-Palooza and her family. Honey loves being in the spotlight. Is there a way to use that to help her get used to the harness?

 If you try teaching her a trick, turn to page 70.

 If you decorate the harness so that Honey will want to show it off, turn to page 33.

That night in your dorm room at Brightstar House, you look up skijoring online. You pull up some photos of dogs pulling people on skis. You've skied before, so you should be able to learn the sport quickly. And it looks as if the dog harness and commands are similar to dogsledding, so the lessons you've already had with Honey won't go to waste.

You check the clock. It's still early enough to call the Rojases to see what they think about skijoring.

Mr. Rojas answers, and when you explain the sport to him, he sounds interested. "Let me talk with my family and give you a call back," he says.

About fifteen minutes later, the phone rings. It's Mrs. Rojas saying that skijoring sounds like fun—Honey should love it!

As you crawl into bed, you have mixed feelings. A part of you wonders if you gave up too soon on dogsledding. But you're also proud that you found another way to get outside, try something new, and spend time with Honey. You fall asleep imagining the feeling of flying along a snowy trail, just you and Honey.

Turn to page 34.

As if to demonstrate, Honey jumps up and puts her paws on Isabel's chest. "Down!" you scold, but instead of obeying, she springs toward the lake, dragging you with her. Without slowing, she dives into the water, splashing your legs. "Honey!" you exclaim, exasperated.

"She sure is a strong puller," Isabel says, giggling. "It looks like she's walking *you*."

"She tires me out before I can tire *her* out," you complain as you lead Honey away from the lake.

Isabel laughs. "I know what you mean," she says. "I have to tire out our family's collie by throwing a tennis ball." She pulls one from her backpack. Honey instantly spies it, and her eyes light up.

"I think Honey needs to learn to pay attention to *you*," Riley says. "When I want to get my dog's attention, I use a strong voice."

You're tempted to borrow Isabel's tennis ball, but you see Riley's point, too. What do you try?

 If you throw a tennis ball with Honey, turn to page 32.

 If you try a firm voice with Honey, turn to page 43.

The van stops below the highest peak of Sky-High Mountain. Ski trails wind down it like white ribbons. When the van door opens, you feel a shiver of excitement mixed with the chill of cold air. You can't wait to get started!

The driver helps all the girls unload their gear. Waving good-bye, Paige heads to the cross-country ski-trail area. Shelby takes off with some of the other girls.

You, Emmy, and Becca hurry to the rental kiosk. Becca groans when she sees the long line. "It'll take forever to get your stuff," she says as she edges toward the slopes.

"Go ahead," you tell her. "I'll meet you as soon as I can."

Becca flashes you a grateful smile as she disappears into the crowd. Emmy stays put by your side. "I'll wait with you," she says. "My lesson doesn't start for half an hour."

When you finally get your equipment, Emmy shows you how to put on your boots. "The boots buckle into the binding on the snowboard," she tells you. "But first you have to decide if you are regular or goofy."

You give her a puzzled look.

Emmy laughs. "I think you need to sign up for a lesson, too," she says. "Then *regular* and *goofy* will make sense."

You probably *should* take a lesson, except you already told Becca you'd meet her at the snowboard park. And she did say she'd teach you.

 If you take a lesson with Emmy, turn to page 50.

 If you find Becca at the park, turn to page 36.

"Thanks for the ideas!" you tell Isabel and Riley. "Mind if I borrow your tennis ball, Isabel? I'm going to try your idea first."

"Sure, no problem," says Isabel, tossing you the ball. Instantly, Honey's ears prick.

You lead Honey to an empty spot on the campus lawn and bend down to unhook her leash. You probably should ask her owners for permission to let her off the leash, but you don't know if you can reach them—and you don't want to take the time to walk back to Pet-Palooza.

After unhooking the leash, you throw the ball. "Fetch," you command—and you notice that your voice *does* sound kind of squeaky.

Honey chases the ball, brings it back, and drops it at your feet. You make her sit before you throw it again—and she does!

Suddenly a squirrel scampers across Honey's path. Ignoring the ball, Honey makes a beeline for the squirrel, which darts toward a tree.

Turn to page 40.

"I think I have the perfect idea," you tell Amber. "I need to jazz up Honey's harness. Since she likes to show off, a fancy 'outfit' might do the trick."

"I know who can help us with *fancy*," Amber says.

"Isabel!" the two of you chime at the same time.

You find your friend Isabel in her room, braiding her curly red hair with ribbons—just what you need! When you explain the situation and ask for her help, she holds up a pink ribbon, smiles teasingly, and asks, "So, what's Honey's favorite color?"

Together, you, Amber, and Isabel tie ribbons into bows on Honey's harness, making sure that the decorations will stay on the pup and not get in her way.

The next afternoon at Pet-Palooza, you find Honey in the play area with Pepper. Crouching, you slip the harness onto her. Then you and Amber clap and make a fuss over how pretty she looks.

Honey doesn't budge. She gives you a puzzled look and then shakes, as if trying to get rid of the harness.

Oh, boy, you think. *Honey hates it!* This was the *silliest* of your silly ideas.

Turn to page 37.

Jen promises to teach you how to skijor, but first she wants you to watch the sport while she demonstrates with her dog, Dare. Amber comes, too, to see what skijoring is all about.

First Jen puts a harness on Dare. Then she puts on her helmet and a special belt around her own waist. She hooks the harness to the belt with a towline.

Dare whines eagerly, ready to go, but Jen makes him sit until she's ready with her skis and poles. Then she says, "Let's go!" and the two are off.

Dare pulls Jen along the loop around the school while she skis behind him. She uses her poles occasionally for balance, but she and Dare seem to be in perfect sync.

"Who's ready to try?" Jen asks when they come flying back. They make it look so easy that you immediately holler, "I am!"

Jen hands you her skijor belt, and you put it on, along with your helmet. When you reach for your ski poles, Jen shakes her head. "Try it without the poles first," she says, "until you get used to working with Dare and the towline."

You nod eagerly, ready to get started. You know how to ski, and Dare follows commands like a champ. This should be a snap!

 Turn to page 52.

As much as you'd like to improve your own dog-training skills, you want Honey to get the training she needs first. "When should we start?" you ask.

"Let's meet at Pet-Palooza tomorrow," Amber suggests.

The next day, you hurry to Pet-Palooza after math class. Honey is alone in the play area taking a nap. She leaps up when she sees you and gives you a warm welcome.

Amber isn't here yet, so you hook the leash onto Honey's collar and practice a few basic commands: whoa, gee, and haw. Honey listens well—until Amber opens the door and brings Pepper into the play area. Immediately, Honey starts barking. You have to keep a tight grip on her leash to keep her from pouncing on poor Pepper.

Fortunately, Pepper is pretty good at tuning out Honey. He focuses on Amber, who gives him the sit command.

"Let's get Honey harnessed," Amber says. "Maybe then we can get her attention, too."

It takes both of you to harness the squirming Honey and Pepper together, side by side. As Amber gives Pepper commands, Honey has no choice but to trot alongside him.

"Your turn," Amber says.

When you take over the lead, you soon have the two dogs walking out the door and down the sidewalk. The plan works!

 Turn to page 39.

Waving good-bye to Emmy, you carry your board to the park. You spot Becca's red helmet in the crowd of snowboarders whizzing over moguls and jumping onto rails. They're also falling—a lot.

You gulp. You're about to turn back and follow Emmy when Becca flies toward you. At the last moment, she zigzags to a stop, spraying snow everywhere.

"Ready for your first lesson?" she asks.

"Well, Emmy showed me how to strap on the board. But I don't know if I'm goofy or regular," you say, trying to pretend that you know what you're talking about.

"That's easy to figure out. Run and slide in the snow," Becca tells you. You give her an odd look, but you do it.

"See how you led with your left foot?" she asks. "That means you're 'regular,' and your left foot will be forward on the board."

"And I wanted to be goofy," you joke as you strap both boots onto the board, your left foot toward the nose.

When you straighten up, you feel as if you're going to topple over at any second.

"Let's shred!" Becca exclaims as she glides off.

 If you stand in place, not having the faintest idea how to move, turn to page 42.

 If you holler "wait up!" and try to join her, turn to page 46.

Sighing, you reach to take off the harness. "Sorry," you say to Honey. "I guess you don't like our handiwork."

Suddenly Honey darts away and begins to prance around the room. Surprised, you stand back and watch. She struts past Pepper and then heads for the door. Turning, she barks at you as if to say, *Let's go show everyone!*

Isabel grins. "Who can resist ribbons?" she says.

Thinking fast, you pull a towline from the equipment shelf and snap it onto Honey's harness. "This is a great chance to see if she'll 'pull' me while she parades around," you explain to Isabel.

"Great idea," Amber says. "I'll follow with Pepper."

The five of you march from the play area. All the volunteers at Pet-Palooza make a fuss over Honey and Pepper.

Honey is so eager to keep showing off, she trots through the outside door. You pass other girls on campus, all of them cheering and whistling while Honey holds her head high. Your idea was a hit. Next stop—dogsledding.

 Turn to page 63.

"A confident trainer does make for a more confident dog," Amber says. "Working with Pepper might really help you."

You and Amber agree that for the next lesson, you'll work on basics with Pepper while Amber works with a more experienced dog team to learn how to maneuver a bigger sled.

"Okay, Pepper, I'm going to put the harness on you," you say as you squat next to the husky. "At least that's one thing I know how to do." Except you don't. Pepper's harness is a little different from Honey's, and the straps get so twisted that Jen has to straighten them out.

Finally you and Pepper are ready to try a small training sled. At least *Pepper* is ready. You mess up the commands, telling Pepper "gee" instead of "haw" to go left, and shouting "wait!" instead of "whoa!" to stop.

In protest, Pepper sits down in the snow and won't budge.

"Sorry, Pepper," you apologize. "It's not your fault we're doing so badly. I just keep getting mixed up."

Suddenly you realize how Honey must feel. Learning all this new information is mind-boggling. No wonder Honey makes mistakes!

 Turn to page 44.

When you head back to Sky-High, the lesson goes even better than you thought it would. The sun is out, and the snow is soft and light.

Jen helps harness Pepper and Honey to a small sled. You cross your fingers, hoping the sled doesn't frighten Honey, but she stands still, following Pepper's lead.

Jen mushes first, climbing onto the sled and using an encouraging voice as she calls commands to the two dogs. Honey bounds along beside Pepper as the sled glides through the snow. Jen makes mushing look so easy and fun that you can hardly wait to try!

Amber takes the next turn, flying away in the sled behind the two dogs. When she finishes, her cheeks are flushed. "Woo-hoo!" she says. "That was awesome."

"My turn!" you exclaim as you hurry toward the sled.

"Why don't you ride with Amber first?" Jen suggests.

"Cool idea—then you can get the feel of how the team works," Amber agrees.

Their comments stop you in your tracks. Don't they have confidence in you?

 If you decide that it's a good idea to mush with Amber, turn to page 45.

 If you decide to prove that you can take the dogs out alone, turn to page 47.

"Honey, *come!*" you call, but she ignores you and races after the squirrel.

You groan with frustration as you run after Honey. She's getting exercise all right—chasing the squirrel, not the ball.

When the squirrel reaches the tree, Honey rises up on her hind legs, her front legs on the tree trunk, and *woofs* up at the squirrel. You reach for her collar, but she darts away.

This isn't working, you realize. Honey thinks it's a game. You've got to figure out a way to catch her—and fast.

You grab the ball. Kneeling, you hold it up and call, "Look, Honey, the ball! Come chase it. *Come.*"

Wagging her fluffy tail, Honey trots over. *"Sit,"* you say, and amazingly, she does. Her tongue is hanging out, so you know that she's finally as tired as you are.

Sighing, you give her a pat and hook the leash to her collar. Your idea did work, sort of. Honey is tired—and she's listening. Next time, you'll throw the ball in the yard at Pet-Palooza. Then Honey—and you—might be ready to try the next step: dogsledding!

⭐ Turn to page 20.

"Wait, Becca!" you call. "I need help." But Becca has disappeared into the crowd.

"I'll help," someone offers. You turn to see a girl on skate skis. You don't recognize her, but then she lifts her goggles to the top of her helmet. Shelby!

"I'm not as good a boarder as Becca," she says with a smile. "But I know enough to get you started."

"Thanks, Shelby," you say warmly. Shelby is always there to help her friends. You're lucky that she was nearby, or who knows how long you might have stayed stuck?

For the next hour, Shelby patiently instructs you—on the bunny slope, where you should have been to start with. Soon you realize that you've got a knack for snowboarding. By the end of the afternoon, you're zipping beside Shelby on her skate skis.

Later, you and Shelby meet up with Becca, Emmy, and Paige. As the five of you walk to the chalet, everyone has fun stories to tell. So do you! Okay, maybe they're about catching air on the *bunny* slope, but you had to start somewhere.

Turn to page 72.

"Come on, Honey, let's walk, ple-e-ease," you beg.

"Wow, *that* was a firm command," Riley says, joking.

Suddenly Honey leaps forward and plunges into the lake, soaking you, Isabel, and Riley. "Honey!" you cry, this time sounding frustrated instead of firm. Honey races back out of the water, but then she flops in the mud along the shoreline and rolls, kicking her legs in the air.

Riley and Isabel burst out laughing, but you don't. It's going to take hours to groom Honey before the Rojases pick her up. You wanted to spend the afternoon *training*, not cleaning her.

But it's your fault. You were looking for a fast way to tire out Honey so that she'd be more trainable. Only there is no shortcut. You're going to have to start from the beginning, ask for help, and be strong enough to stay the course.

"Okay, Riley," you say to your friend. "How about some tips on using a firm, commanding voice?"

The End

For a solid week, you go to Pet-Palooza every day after school to work with Pepper. Finally, by Friday, you feel as if you've mastered the harness and the commands without a sled. Only then do you start working with Honey again.

Knowing what you are doing and being clear with commands gives both you *and* Honey more confidence. Soon she's used to the harness. She gets better at following commands on the leash, too.

"Are you ready for the next step?" Amber asks. When you nod eagerly, she says, "We need to teach Honey how to pull." She holds up a towline and a special belt for you to wear. "You can use this to teach her without snow."

Amber hooks Honey's harness to the towline and shows you how to put the belt around your waist. Then she hooks the towline to your belt as if you were the sled.

Amber and Pepper, wearing the same equipment, run ahead. Honey chases them while you run behind her. You can feel how strong she is!

As you call commands, Honey does a pretty good job of listening to you. Even after Amber quits running, Honey continues on until both of you are panting.

 Turn to page 48.

You wish you were ready to mush on your own, but you know that you still have a lot to learn. You take Amber up on her invitation to ride the sled together.

You and Amber balance side-by-side on the sled runners. Since the dogs are pulling both of you, Amber starts them off slowly. She calls commands confidently, and the dogs respond right away.

How did Amber get so good so fast? you wonder. *Oh, right. She didn't have to deal with Miss Honey!* But then you remind yourself that Honey is learning from Pepper, just as you're learning from Amber.

Amber shows you how to brake and how to steer by shifting your weight left and right on the runners. She lets you try some commands, too. "Gee," you call when you want the dogs to go right, and "on by!" when a rabbit darts across the path. Mushing is so much fun that you grin from ear to ear until your cheeks are stiff with the cold. If you weren't holding so tightly to the handlebars, you'd reach over and give Amber a high five.

By the time you've circled the sled back to the school, you feel as if you're ready to handle an Arctic expedition.

"Dogsledding is awesome!" you tell Jen when the team slows down beside her. "And you were right to send me out with Amber first," you admit as you jump off the sled. "Learning how to mush takes time. Pepper and Honey are stronger together, and Amber and I were, too!"

The End

Becca heads down a gentle slope, which shouldn't be too tricky. You've skied way bigger hills than this before. But you had *poles* to help you balance, and your skis moved independently. Right now, you feel as if you're nailed to a board that's glued to the snowy ground. How do you even get started?

You try to copy the position of a girl coming past you. You flex your front knee and lean forward, pointing one arm out in front of you. As you turn your upper body toward the nose of the board, you begin to move through the snow.

Your pulse races. This is fun! Then you hit a rough patch. Your legs wobble as the board picks up speed. *Whoa, not so fun.*

Throwing out your arms as if you were on a tightrope, you try to regain your balance.

"Press your heel edge into the snow!" Becca hollers.

Heel edge? You have no idea what she means. The board weaves crazily, and you realize that not only do you not know what a "heel edge" is, but you also never learned how to stop!

Turn to page 76.

"I'm ready to try it on my own," you say confidently. Amber glances toward Jen, who thinks for a moment and then nods toward the sled. "Okay, climb on," she says, "but take this with you." Jen pulls a small map from her pocket and hands it to you.

"Don't go off the dog trails," Jen warns. "You might get stuck in deep snow or run into cross-country skiers."

Eager to get going, you fold the map and stuff it into your jacket pocket. "Don't worry. I'll keep my eye out for the dog-trail signs," you assure her. Actually, you don't want to hear Jen's warnings. Too many of them might sink your courage, and you want to show your friends that you can do this.

When you're settled on the sled, you call, "Let's go!" The two eager dogs start loping down the trail. The chilly wind brushes your cheeks, and snow kicks onto your boots. The only sound is the *zing* of the runners on the snow and the panting of the dogs.

Incredible! you think, and for a moment, your heart pounds as you pretend you're racing in the Junior Iditarod.

Turn to page 49.

The next afternoon, you and Honey try the towline on your own around the campus trails. It's a blast!

Later, when the Rojas family stops by to pick up Honey, she's so tired that even Russ can easily take her by the leash.

"I've never seen Honey behave so well!" exclaims Mrs. Rojas. "What's your secret?"

You do a show-and-tell with the harness and towline. It turns out that both Mr. and Mrs. Rojas enjoy jogging and want to learn how to run with Honey in the harness. That way, they can all exercise together.

You pat yourself on the back, proud that you were strong enough to stick with training. One day Honey may be a pretty good sled dog, but you've already met a more important goal. You found a way for her family to give her lots of exercise and love—just what Honey needs.

The End

Up ahead, the trail forks. You spot the dog-trail sign on the right-hand trail.

"Haw!" you holler. Pepper, who is acting as lead dog, instantly turns left. "No, Pepper! Haw!"

He continues left, loping down the trail with Honey running happily beside him. Why is Pepper disobeying?

Then it hits you: "Haw" means "go left." The husky isn't disobeying. He's following the orders you gave him—the *wrong* orders.

You're scolding yourself when you hear the whine of a motor behind you. Startled, you glance at a sign marking the side of the path. A snowmobile is painted on it.

Fear clutches your insides. You've taken the snowmobile path instead of the dogsledding trail!

 If you try to move the sled off the trail, turn to page 53.

 If you try to stop, turn to page 112.

As you watch a snowboarder zoom down the halfpipe, you realize again that snowboarding is a *lot* different from skiing.

"A lesson is a good idea," you tell Emmy.

"Lessons start in ten minutes," Emmy says. "We'd better sign you up."

You glance toward the crowded snowboard park. There's no way you can find Becca to tell her you're going with Emmy. You hope she'll understand.

"I've already learned the basics," Emmy tells you, "so I'm taking an advanced lesson."

You definitely *aren't* advanced, so you sign up for the beginner's group. But it turns out that the beginner's group is filled with kids half your age—and size. You'll stick out like an ostrich in a snowsuit!

"You know, maybe I'll join your group," you say as you hurry after Emmy. "I'm a pretty good skier, so I should be okay."

The advanced group is lined up near a chairlift. "We're taking the lift to the top of Falling Star," says the instructor.

A ski trail? Already? You stare up the slope to the top of Falling Star. It's a long way up—and down—and you don't even know yet if you're regular or goofy!

 If you convince yourself you can handle it, turn to page 55.

 If you go back to the beginner's group, turn to page 69.

Jen hooks the towline to your belt. She walks with you down the trail while you try out your commands: "Gee. Haw. On by." Dare is well trained and listens to you, so Jen steps away and lets you go on ahead without her.

Quickly, you find out how strong Dare is. Faster and faster he pulls you along the snowy path. "Easy. Easy!" you call, and he does slow down. But then the trail curves down a slope.

Jen showed you how to snowplow so that you don't go faster than your dog and run into him. But Dare is so strong, he keeps dragging you forward. "If you get into trouble, ski to the side of Dare," you remember Jen saying. You snowplow to the right of a bush. Dare runs to the left.

"Whoa!" you holler—too late. You and the towline wrap around the bush, and Dare stops abruptly. Losing your balance, you plop face-first into the snow.

That was graceful! Quickly, you look up to see if Dare is all right. He's staring down at you with his tongue hanging out—*laughing at me,* you think. Awkwardly you get back up on your skis.

 If you decide that skijoring is too out-of-control for you to try with Honey, turn to page 54.

 If you decide that by practicing more with Dare, you can do this, turn to page 56.

You have to get off this path and find the dogsledding trail before the snowmobile zooms up behind you. But how?

Thick woods line the trail on the right. There is an open brushy space on the left, but immediately beyond is a mass of boulders. If you steer into the woods, you'll probably run into a tree. But if you steer left, you might run into the rocks.

Behind you, the whine turns to a roar. Your heart pounds. You need to make a decision fast!

Suddenly Pepper makes a sharp right onto another fork on the trail, dragging Honey and the sled with him. You spot the marker that shows a dog pulling a sled. It's as if Pepper read the sign and knew this was a safe trail!

"Good boy, Pepper!" you holler as the sled flies down the path.

For just a moment, you're flying high with relief. But as you circle the team back toward Sky-High Dog School, fear begins creeping its way back into your heart.

You just put yourself and your sled dogs in a whole lot of danger, and now you have to work up the courage to admit to Amber and Jen that you were wrong to head out alone. Until you're smart enough to read the map and follow a trail, you won't be doing solo sledding again any time soon.

The End

Shivering, you take off your gloves. Your fingers are frozen, and you have snow down your collar and your boots.

Dare gives you a lick, but it doesn't make you feel much better. *I guess snow sports just aren't for me—or Honey,* you think sadly.

When you picture the cute retriever in your mind, though, you start to smile. Maybe just spending time with Honey is what you need, not conquering a new sport.

Taking off your skis, you head back down the trail, walking beside Dare this time. By the time you reach Amber and Jen, you've made up your mind. You hope your friends won't be too disappointed.

"Um, I think skijoring isn't for me," you say reluctantly. "And dogsledding isn't for Honey. Maybe she and I need to focus on hanging out and having fun on campus instead."

"Hey, that's okay," Jen says cheerfully as she takes Dare from you. "Snow sports aren't for every girl—or every dog. You tried your best. Be proud of that."

Amber nods, too. "And because of you, I learned about a new sport. I think I might give this skijoring thing a try."

You smile with relief. "Thanks," you say. "Now I'm ready to change into dry clothes—and go see Honey!"

 Turn to page 57.

After a deep breath and a little coaching by Emmy, you get onto the ski lift with one boot bound to the board and one boot free. The lift carries you over the snowboard park, where you spot Becca's red helmet. You and Emmy holler and wave. Becca looks up, but she frowns and doesn't wave back. *Uh-oh.* She must be mad that you aren't at the park with her.

"Look, there's the campus!" Emmy says, nudging you. At the bottom of the mountain, Innerstar U is a patch of green dotted with buildings. As you and Emmy search for Brightstar House, the lift carries you uphill, and suddenly you're at the top. You manage to get off the lift without wiping out.

You and Emmy hurry over to the instructor, who is giving tips on how to *traverse.* "As you go downhill, you want to control your speed by traveling diagonally across the slope instead of straight down," he says. "Ready to follow me?"

You nod, but Emmy must see the confusion on your face. "Place your weight on the front foot and turn your body toward the nose," she says. "That will get you moving. Then traverse by moving your board at an angle."

Miraculously, you begin to slide forward at a slant. "Are you good to go?" Emmy asks.

 If you tell Emmy you're "good to go," turn to page 60.

 If you tell Emmy you need H-E-L-P, turn to page 59.

Brushing off the snow, you walk back to Jen and Amber, leading Dare behind you. "What happened?" Jen asks.

"Um . . ." Your face turns red—and not just from the chilly air. You confess that you started skiing too fast and had to veer to the side of Dare so that you wouldn't hit him.

"That's exactly what you should have done," Jen says. "Or you could have used a hockey stop."

"Hockey stop?" Amber repeats.

You're curious, too. "Can you show us?" you ask.

Jen demonstrates how to stop quickly. As she glides down a hill toward you, she turns her body and skis sideways while bending her knees. Snow sprays in the air, and she stops immediately.

You practice the move and then try it while hooked behind Dare. It works!

Soon you and Dare are zipping up and down hills— with your ski poles. You even handle the "come around" command without falling over.

The day is a success! Amber is even intrigued enough to want to try the sport with Pepper. As for you, you can't wait to try skijoring with Honey. You grin as you picture the retriever flying down the trail, leading you on skis behind her.

 Turn to page 58.

When you get back to campus, you quickly change and hang up your snow gear to dry. Will you wear it again this season? Maybe. But right now, you want to see Honey.

You jog to Pet-Palooza, and when you get there, Honey barks a greeting. She's just as happy to see you!

"Come on, girl, let's do something we both love to do," you say. You pick up a ball from the bin of toys, and Honey's eyes light up. Dancing in place, she lets out an excited *woof.*

You lead her to the outside play area, and for ten minutes, you throw the ball for her. She retrieves it, drops it at your feet, and sits, ready for you to throw it again.

Laughing, you pat her soft head. "This *is* your favorite sport, isn't it?" you say. "No wonder you weren't crazy about pulling a sled."

Afterward you take Honey for a walk and then brush her silky coat. Later, when the Rojases come to pick her up, she'll be groomed and happily worn out.

You were glad you tried dogsledding and skijoring. But you also feel good that you were strong enough to make a different choice—one that was right for *you* and your new friend, Honey.

The End

The next day after classes, you work with Honey at Pet-Palooza. You want her to be comfortable with the harness and towline before trying them with skis.

Honey doesn't mind the harness this time, and she likes being hooked up to you. But instead of running ahead of you as Dare did, she wants to turn and give you kisses.

Your friend Shelby, who is volunteering at the pet day-care center, watches you. "What are you doing?" she asks.

You explain skijoring and then add, "I want Honey to pull me forward, but she's not sure what to do."

Shelby cocks her head, letting her gaze drift toward the other dogs in the play area. Chocolate Chip, a young Labrador retriever, is chewing on a toy. When she sees him, Shelby perks up. "I've got an idea," she says.

Shelby puts Chocolate Chip on a leash and leads him in front of Honey, who quickly follows them. Soon the four of you are walking along the sidewalk outside Pet-Palooza. Honey moves eagerly in front of you, keeping the towline taut. You pretend you're wearing skis and practice giving her commands.

"That looks like fun!" Shelby says when you stop to praise Honey. "I love to ski. I wonder if Chocolate Chip and I could take lessons, too?"

"Maybe you can!" you exclaim.

Shelby says she'll check with Chocolate Chip's owners. You cross your fingers, hoping they'll say yes.

 Turn to page 62.

"I'm good to go," you tell Emmy, "except down that steep hill!"

Emmy laughs. "Don't worry," she says. "I'll ride beside you the whole way."

Sighing with relief, you relax a little. Emmy is a pretty good instructor. She shows you how to do a heelside turn and a toeside turn. You fall a lot at first, but you practice until you can do the moves with confidence.

Then, using the turns, you head down Falling Star, carving an S as you glide. It takes forever to reach the bottom, but you notice that you're not the only one from the lesson who is taking her time. Finally you and Emmy reach the bottom. The instructor gathers the group and congratulates everyone on a good run down the slope.

You're giving Emmy a high five when Becca rides up. Stopping abruptly, she glares at you. "I thought you came to board with *me*," she says. It's not a question, so at first you stare at her, your mouth open, not sure how to respond.

 Turn to page 65.

You stick up your thumb. "Good to go," you tell Emmy. The truth is, you don't have a clue what you're doing, but you don't want to hold Emmy back.

"Are you sure you don't want me to stay with you?" Emmy asks, glancing down the trail. The instructor is waving for the two of you to follow.

"Go on. I'll be right behind you," you tell her. "*Way* behind you" is more like it, but you don't say that out loud.

As Emmy heads down the hill, you practice shifting your weight to your front foot, just as she showed you. The snowboard glides forward smoothly, and you feel a rush of exhilaration. But too soon the board picks up speed. You wish you had spent more time practicing the traverse, because now you're heading straight downhill—fast.

Suddenly a group of girls snowboard directly in front of you. You need to do something *right now,* or you're going to plow into them!

 If you quickly shift your weight so that you head away from the girls, turn to page 64.

 If you panic and fall to avoid them, turn to page 67.

The next weekend at Sky-High, you're excited to have Shelby and Chocolate Chip by your side. Amber and Pepper are there, too.

When your lesson begins, you can tell right away that your work with Honey on campus has paid off. She eagerly pulls you down the snowy path that loops around the school. Chocolate Chip takes to skijoring pretty quickly, too, as if he's done it before.

"You're *all* doing so well," Jen says at the third lesson, on Sunday. "Maybe we should skijor a longer trail together."

She leads you to the start of a nature trail. It's a frosty, blue-sky day, and winding around the mountain loop is exhilarating. You hate to see the trail end, and you can tell your friends feel the same way.

"Maybe we should form a skijor club," Shelby suggests.

"Oooh, I like that idea," Amber chimes in. "We could even train together for a skijor race—a fun, easy one."

Shelby frowns. "I don't know if I'm ready for racing," she says. "How about a longer skijor trip on the mountain? There are miles of trails."

Your friends look at you, waiting for you to weigh in.

If you vote for a skijor trip on the mountain, turn to page 88.

If you vote for a skijoring race, go online to innerstarU.com/secret and enter this code: URSTRONG

You can't wait for your next dogsledding lesson. As you, Honey, Pepper, and Amber hop the van to Sky-High, Amber says, "I see you left the bows on Honey's harness."

"Yeah," you reply. "I hope the other dogs won't laugh too hard when I put it on her!"

Finally the van rumbles to a stop in front of the school. Jen is already there with a team of dogs hooked to a sled. Honey leaps out eagerly, but when the dogs begin howling, she tucks her tail and quickly jumps back into the van.

"Come on," you cajole, holding out a cheese treat. "Pepper's out here. He's not scared."

Honey thumps her tail, but she doesn't move. You don't have a clue what to do next. Oh, you wish you were a more confident trainer!

 If you look for ways to help Honey conquer her fear, turn to page 66.

 If you tackle your own worry first, turn to page 68.

"Watch out!" you holler. Shifting your weight, you pivot the nose of the board, barely missing the group of girls.

Heart pounding, you wait until the board comes to a halt. Then you undo the bindings on the board so that you can pull your boots out and *walk* downhill. You're done snowboarding—at least until after you take an actual lesson.

When you finally make it to the bottom of Falling Star Trail, Emmy runs up to you, carrying her board, too. "There you are!" she says. "How'd it go? Did you have fun?"

You're trembling with fatigue. Your first snowboarding experience was *not* fun. In fact, it was dangerous. It was only luck that kept you from causing an accident.

"Not so fun," you tell Emmy, your voice shaky. "I almost ran into a whole pack of skiers. I need to go back to the beginner's group."

 Turn to page 69.

Then you realize that Becca is more *hurt* than angry. And you can't blame her—you went off with Emmy instead of meeting Becca at the snowboard park.

"I'm sorry, but I needed a lesson before I could keep up with you," you explain. "Watching tricks on a video game isn't the same as learning real ones, you know?"

"I guess," Becca says, her mouth still drooping.

"Are you two ready to head to the chalet?" Emmy asks.

"It is getting late," you say, noticing that the sun is setting and your gloves are frozen. "And we have all day tomorrow to hit the slopes," you say to Becca.

Becca shrugs. "Okay. I *am* getting hungry," she says, starting to sound like her old self again.

After turning in your equipment, you walk toward the cute, Swiss-style cabins strung along the hill like tree lights.

"Wait up, guys!" you hear. Paige is hurrying toward you carrying her cross-country skis. Her parka and snow pants are damp. "Um, I had a few spills," she admits.

You laugh. "I'm glad I'm not the only one who spent the afternoon falling," you say.

 Turn to page 84.

You and Honey have been working so hard. You aren't going to give up now. "I think Honey is ready to try a training sled," you say to Amber and Jen. "But for some reason, the team of dogs is freaking her out."

Jen nods. "What if the van driver takes you to a quieter place?" she suggests. "I could meet you there with a sled."

Amber and Pepper climb back into the van, and Jen instructs the driver where to go. The van winds up the road and parks. You spy Jen trotting down a trail toward you with a sled. Honey sees her, too, and jumps out of the van.

"Let's hook her up beside Pepper," Jen says. "He'll give her confidence." She helps you and Amber get the two dogs harnessed and attached to the sled.

Jen rides the sled, since she's the most experienced. You and Amber march ahead of the dogs. "It's a parade!" Amber cheers. Pepper seems confused by the fanfare but listens to Jen's commands. Honey gets right into the fun, and soon she's pulling confidently, too.

"Ready to get closer to the other dogs?" Jen asks.

Your stomach flutters, but you nod and start marching back toward the school. The howling of the dogs grows louder. Gradually you march closer and closer to the school until you can see the dog team. Instead of turning tail, Honey follows Pepper past them, her tail waving like a flag.

The instructor and other students laugh as Honey struts by in her fancy harness, but hey, it's working!

 Turn to page 68.

You'd better bail before you hit someone. Fortunately, you remember from ski lessons how to fall safely. You let yourself drop backward, tucking your chin and arms. The snow is icy, and you hit with a *thud*. You're moving so fast, you continue sliding crazily down the hill—right into the path of another boarder, who swerves at the last minute.

"Sorry, sorry!" you call when you finally stop on a rough patch of snow.

You're afraid the snowboarder is going to holler at you, and you can't blame her. But when the snowboarder lifts her googles, you realize it's Becca!

"I *thought* that was you flying wildly down the slope," she says, laughing. "Cool move!"

You shake your head. "*Not* so cool," you tell her. "I was out of control. I should have taken a lesson."

"I can show you a few things," Becca says. But her gaze darts toward the snowboard park, and you know she'd rather be there—not babysitting you.

This time, you're strong and smart enough to say, "Thanks, Becca. But I really need a serious lesson. Afterward, I'll join you at the snowboard park. And when I get there, I'll show you how well I can stop!"

The End

Jen and the lead instructor meet you back at the school. "Okay," says Jen, "now it's *your* turn to develop some confidence. You need to be a good musher for Honey, and that means practicing how to drive a dog team."

Your nervousness grows as the instructor says that she'll pull you on a sled behind a slow-moving snowmobile. "You'll get the feel of the sled without worrying about the dogs," she explains.

"I started out that way, too," Amber says encouragingly. "It's fun! And I'll take care of Honey for you."

As Amber takes the harnesses off Honey and Pepper, Jen shows you how to lean right and left on the sled and how to put one foot down to brake. "Ready to try it?" she asks after a while.

You swallow hard and nod. The instructor gives you a thumbs-up and climbs onto the snowmobile. As the snowmobile starts up, you grasp the handlebars of the sled and put your feet on the runners. In no time, you're gliding slowly behind the snowmobile. Bending your legs and body slightly, you sway right and left to keep the sled balanced around turns.

I can do this, you think to yourself as the snowmobile slowly circles back toward the school. *I can really do this!*

🌟 Turn to page 77.

Telling Emmy good-bye, you trudge to the beginner's lesson. You're late, but the instructor spends a little extra time with you to make sure that by the end of the lesson, you've mastered the basics: sideslipping, riding fakie (backward), stopping, and gliding straight. You also learn how to fall safely and get back up—tricks you could have used on Falling Star Trail!

When you turn in your rental board, you spot Emmy and Becca. They're talking excitedly about the adventures they had.

"After my lesson, I went down Falling Star again," Emmy says. "Much faster the second time!"

"And I mastered a three-hundred-sixty-degree spin," says Becca, twirling in the air.

"Wow. You guys are awesome," you say, meaning it.

"Hey, I thought you were with Emmy all afternoon," Becca says, looking kind of hurt.

"Nope. I was with Jake and Kelsey and the other seven-year-olds," you joke.

Now that you've taken a beginner's lesson, you realize that you're not ashamed to talk about it. In fact, you're proud of being strong enough to swallow your pride and stay safe. And who knows? After a good night's sleep at the chalet, you may be ready to tackle a more advanced lesson, too—and that three-sixty spin!

The End

You decide to teach Honey a new trick. If she catches on quickly, you'll know more about what she likes to do, which might help you train her to pull a sled, too.

You have your opportunity at Sky-High the next weekend, after a fresh snowfall. The snow is wet, and when you scoop up a handful in your mitten, you discover that the snow packs well into a ball. Honey's eyes are glued to that ball of snow, as if she's waiting for you to throw it.

"Great idea," you say with a grin. You toss Honey the snowball, which she catches easily. Then you make her sit still as you slowly step backward away from her. When you're about ten feet away, you toss another snowball, which she catches.

"Wow. Honey's better than a baseball player!" says Amber, clapping and cheering.

Now you know that Honey *does* enjoy being trained.

"Why don't we try the harness again," you tell Amber. "This time when we put it on her, we'll make it seem as if we're teaching her a trick."

Turn to page 73.

That night as you settle into your bunk bed at the chalet, Becca says from the bunk above, "The snowboarding park is getting boring. Let's all do Lightning Bolt tomorrow."

"Isn't that an advanced trail?" you ask as you snuggle deeper under your comfy quilt.

Shelby frowns as she plumps up her pillow. "Count me out," she says. "I'm just starting to get the hang of skate skis."

"I'm not ready to try it either," Emmy says from the bunk above Shelby.

"We can *all* do the Bolt," Becca insists. "It's not much harder than the bunny slope."

"I'll try it," you pipe up, a little reluctantly. But you do owe Becca one since you didn't board with her today.

In the bed across from you, Shelby is still frowning. You prop yourself up on one arm and say to her, "Come on, Shelb. We were *zooming* down that bunny slope this afternoon."

Shelby grins at you. "We kind of were, weren't we?" she says. "All right," she adds with a sigh. "I'm in."

"Yes!" You wish everyone good night, and as you fall asleep, lightning bolts flash across your dreams.

Turn to page 74.

"Sit, Honey. Shake," you say encouragingly. You get her to shake first with one paw, then the other. "Good girl," you praise, and as she lifts her paws, you slip on the harness.

Straightening, you clap and say, "What a beautiful girl!" As you and Honey march around in a circle, she seems to totally forget the harness. She prances, lifting one paw after the other. Amber laughs and cheers.

"Good for you," she says after the lesson, "for staying strong and not giving up on your furry friend."

You smile proudly. All this time Honey was telling you what she liked and how to train her. You just needed to listen. With Honey's help, you'll figure out a way to conquer *each* new step. Soon she'll be pulling a sled—or performing new tricks for the Rojases. Either is perfectly fine with you.

The End

Staying strong means not giving up on your friends.

The next morning Becca wakes you up by singing, "Lightning Bolt, here we come!"

You and Shelby glance at each other. "We're going to do the Bolt, right?" you ask her.

She nods, but she doesn't look very excited.

"Woo-hoo!" Becca hollers. "Hurry up and let's go!"

Later, when you rent your snowboard, Shelby hands you a pocket-sized tool kit. "We should carry these in case our bindings come loose," she says solemnly.

You nod, your nerves jumping at the thought of a problem. And as the chairlift takes you, Shelby, and Becca to the top of the mountain, you begin to wonder if you're really ready for Lightning Bolt.

As the lift passes over the trail, the slope zigzags beneath you, branching off to two slopes about halfway down. Shelby sucks in her breath. "I'm not ready for this," she whispers.

Becca, however, turns around from the chair in front of you and exclaims, "Wow, it's just like the trail in the video game!"

Turn to page 80.

You lose your balance, and your weight shifts forward onto the front edge of the board. It digs into the snow, stopping abruptly. You fly forward, executing a perfect face plant into a snowdrift.

Coughing and sputtering, you lift up your head. Snow sticks to your eyelashes, cheeks, and chin. The snow is soft and nothing hurts, but your arms are stuck in the drift and your legs are stretched out behind you, with your feet still attached to the board. You have no idea how to push yourself out of the snow or get out of your bindings.

You'd yell for help, but you're too embarrassed.

"Becca?" you croak, hoping your friend will hear you.

 Turn to page 78.

Next step? You ride with Jen on a sled behind a team of dogs. Jen expertly guides the dogs, who race down the trail, barking excitedly. The crisp air whips past, and you're grinning so wide that your teeth get cold.

"It's fun, isn't it?" asks Jen as the team careens around a bend. "But there's a lot that can go wrong, too. The only thing that connects you to the team is the sled."

You can barely nod, you're hanging on so tightly.

Jen hollers "gee," and the team darts down the right-hand trail. "You never want to lose the team," Jen continues. "That means that if you fall off, try to grab ahold of the sled, or the team will keep running."

Don't fall off. Don't lose the sled. "Got it," you say. But you can't help asking, "What happens if the dogs keep running?"

Jen smiles. "Well, you'll be stranded, for one," she says. "And the dogs could end up wrapped around a tree—or worse."

You gulp, wondering about the *worse*. Your teeth begin to chatter as the sun goes behind a cloud. Your knees are shaking, too, they're so tired, and your confidence is starting to falter.

As Jen circles and heads the sled back to the school, you decide you need more practice before trying this on your own or with Honey. Even then, will you ever be strong enough to handle a sled, plus an inexperienced dog?

 Turn to page 79.

An arm reaches around your waist and lifts you to your feet. A teenage girl wearing a ski-patrol jacket and sunglasses frowns at you. "You need to learn how to snow-board on the bunny slope before hitting the park," she says firmly.

Your face turns red—or it would if it weren't covered with snow. "I'm sorry," you say. "My friend was helping me, but she . . ."

You stop yourself. It's not fair to blame Becca. You were the one who decided not to take a lesson. "Um, could you help me unstrap my boots from my bindings?" you ask in a shaky voice.

If the ski-patrol girl weren't wearing sunglasses, you're pretty sure you'd see her rolling her eyes.

After you thank her, you look for Becca to tell her you're going to take a real lesson—the lesson that you should have taken in the first place. You just totally embarrassed yourself, but you're going to shake it off—along with the snow. Tomorrow, after a lesson, you'll be strong enough to try the park again.

The End

By the time you head back to Sky-High for another lesson, you're warmed up and determined not to let your worries get the best of you. The sun shines overhead as Jen and the lead instructor help you practice with a two-dog team. First you practice braking using the sled's brake and dragging a foot. While braking, you call "easy" to slow down and "whoa" to stop.

Next, you steer the dogs around in a figure eight to get the hang of turning. You want to make sure you have these skills perfected before trying the team on a trail. Soon you are weight shifting to steer, balancing well on the sled runners, and commanding the dogs all on your own.

"Tomorrow it's time to try Honey," the instructor says. Amber squeals with excitement. She and Pepper have been going out on short runs and are ready to have you join them.

But you? Um, not so excited, even though you did seem to master some skills today. Honey is inexperienced and unpredictable, and Jen's warnings keep flashing through your head: *Don't fall off. Hang on to the sled. Don't lose the team!*

 Turn to page 83.

The lift drops you off at the tippy-top. Above you is blue sky. Below is a white swath cut through the woods angling to the right and then to the left.

You gulp, and you see Shelby stiffen beside you. "Uh, I'm taking the lift back down," she says suddenly. "Sorry, guys."

You wave good-bye, wondering if you should go with her. But Becca gives a whoop of delight and says, "Glad you're not chicken like Shelby." She lowers her goggles and adjusts her red helmet. "Last one to the bottom buys hot chocolate."

 If you follow Shelby and take the chairlift down, turn to page 82.

 If you blast off with Becca, turn to page 92.

"She's not budging," you tell Amber. "Any suggestions?"

"Hand me your cheese treats," she says.

You pull your baggie from your jacket pocket and toss it to Amber, who takes out several treats. Standing outside the van door, she calls, "Come on, Honey. Let's play!" Pepper barks encouragement, too.

"Look Honey," you say gently, "your friends want you to jump out of the van and play."

Slowly, Honey's tail begins to wag. Suddenly, she jumps from the van, almost dragging you with her. She pulls the leash from your hand and frolics in the snow with Pepper. Then she races up to Amber, who tosses her a cheese treat.

"Step one, getting Honey out of the van: accomplished," you say with a sigh.

Amber laughs, but then you start to worry again. Hooking up Honey to the sled comes next.

It took three of you to convince Honey to leave the van. Is the retriever ready for step two? Or will it take a whole team to get her in the harness?

 Turn to page 86.

"I'd better go with Shelby to make sure she gets to the bottom okay," you say to Becca. "We'll cheer you on from the lift." In reality, you aren't brave enough to do Lightning Bolt either—or to tell Becca the truth about your fear.

Becca shrugs and starts heading down the slope.

Catching up with Shelby, you wait in line to get on the lift with her.

Shelby sighs. "I'm sorry you have to go back with me instead of doing the trail," she says.

That's when you decide to tell Shelby the truth. "I don't want to go down the trail either," you admit. "My gut's telling me I'm not ready to tackle a bolt of lightning."

The two of you smile at each other.

Becca beats you to the bottom, which is no surprise. But as you head to the chalet with your friends, you're proud that you were strong enough to make your own decision about the trail. And as you sip your hot chocolate, you don't even mind listening as Becca tells you—over and over again—how much fun she had conquering the Bolt!

The End

The following day, as the van winds up the mountain, your stomach rolls anxiously. Beside you, Honey pants and whines as if she's getting anxious, too.

When the van stops in front of the school, Pepper and Amber bound out the door from the back seat. "Today will be so much fun!" Amber exclaims.

"Definitely," you reply, trying to sound excited.

Honey peers out the van door as if expecting disaster. You sigh, wishing she was as eager as Pepper is. "Come on, you big baby," you scold. "Out of the van."

Honey cowers a little, picking up on the harsh tone in your voice. When you see her anxious eyes, you feel terrible. You remember how nervous you were yesterday and how everyone was super patient with you. They went over and over each skill until you felt more confident.

Even though you're feeling not-so-confident today, you need to pull yourself together and be a better trainer for Honey.

 If you take a deep breath and give her an encouraging hug, turn to page 110.

 If you enlist Amber's help with Honey, turn to page 81.

Later, as the four of you climb into your bunk beds at the chalet, Becca tells everyone about the snowboard park. "I rode the halfpipe for the first time," she says excitedly. "It felt as if I was flying. Then I nailed a whale tail."

Whale tail? You have no idea what Becca is talking about. Your slow run down Falling Star isn't even close to what she can do at the park.

"That's so different from cross-country skiing," Paige says. "I love gliding along the path, listening to the birds."

Leaning over the edge of the bed above you, Becca whispers, "Snoozeville."

"Cross-country sounds fun," Emmy says. "But I still love the speed of going downhill."

"Me, too. Tomorrow, it's definitely the park again," Becca says. Then she peers down at you again. "Now that you've learned the basics, are you ready to try some tricks?"

You hesitate. One run down Falling Star didn't make you an expert ready for the halfpipe. And every muscle in your body aches. A relaxing day cross-country skiing might be better, except you don't want to disappoint Becca again.

 If you give in to Becca and agree to go boarding the next day, turn to page 90.

 If you decide to chill with Paige on cross-country skis, turn to page 87.

The other dogs and trainers are gathering in front of the dogsledding school. You see Jen and the instructor with their clipboards.

"The lesson's about to begin," Amber says. She and Pepper stride eagerly over to the group. You hook the leash onto Honey's collar, wishing you were as enthusiastic.

"Come, Honey," you say firmly, but Honey must hear anxiety in your voice. Spinning, she turns back toward the van. Fortunately, the door is shut, so she can't jump in.

Using cheese treats, you finally convince Honey to join the lesson. But as soon as Jen brings out the harnesses, Honey flops down in the snow.

"Sit up, Honey," you say, tugging gently upward on the leash. Reluctantly, she gets up. You straddle her to pull the harness over her head, and she plops down again.

Finally, with Jen's help, you get the harness strapped on correctly. But the whole time, Honey's eyes dart worriedly from you to the other dogs.

Amber brings Pepper over, and the two of you silently work to get the dogs hooked up to the sled. You haven't even started sledding, and already you're tired.

"Step three, getting the sled moving forward," you say to Amber. "Pepper may be ready, but I'm not too sure about Honey and me." What you don't tell Amber is that if step three is a bust, you're giving up.

 Turn to page 98.

"I'm not quite ready for the fish tail," you admit to Becca. "I might try cross-country skiing with Paige instead. Is that okay with you?"

"*Whale* tail," Becca corrects. "And it's fine with me," she snaps, sounding not fine at all. You're sorry that Becca is unhappy with your decision, but your body is telling you that it's not ready for a tough challenge so soon.

"It's cool you're going with me," Paige says. "I'm hoping to spot a snowshoe hare. I saw tracks today." She pulls up a picture of the tracks on her digital camera and hops onto your bed to show you.

"You'd rather track a rabbit than perform an aerial one-eighty on a snowboard? Total nap," Becca jokes, not so lightly, from the bunk bed above.

Paige ignores Becca—she's pretty good at that, you've noticed. So you do, too. *I can't always please Becca,* you tell yourself. And Paige is lots of fun to be with.

But as you turn out the lights and crawl under the covers, you wonder, *What if cross-country skiing IS a total nap compared to snowboarding?* There's always a chance that Becca will be right.

Turn to page 104.

You help the other members of your newfound club plan a skijoring trip for next weekend along the Sky-High trails. You're looking forward to exploring the mountain.

The girls put supplies, such as water, snacks, dog booties, and extra gloves, in small packs. Then you map out a trail, leaving a copy with the office at the Sky-High Dog School. You also let the office know when you expect to return, just in case of problems.

After harnessing the eager dogs, you're off! Jen and Dare are in the lead, since they know the trails well. Shelby and Chocolate Chip are next, then Amber and Pepper, and you and Honey bring up the rear.

As you glide along, it begins to snow. Shelby breaks into song: "Doggies pant, are you listening? As we glide, snow is glistening . . . Skiing in a winter wonderland."

Turn to page 91.

Saturday morning, Becca's voice pulls you out of a dream. "Wake up, you gnarly shredders!" she calls. She's standing in the doorway, already dressed even though the sun is barely up.

"Emmy is ready for the whale tail, right, Emmy?" Becca asks. Emmy nods sleepily from her bottom bunk.

"Are you game?" Becca asks you. Her enthusiasm gets you out of your bunk and nodding yes, too. You have to admit, you're even slightly pumped.

After breakfast, you dress and pack up your gear. You say good-bye to the others, and then you, Emmy, and Becca head to the snowboarding park.

"We can start with the halfpipe," Becca says. "For your first time, you just traverse it—you know, riding from the top of one wall and then turning and riding to the top of the other wall."

"Cool," Emmy says, sounding nervous but excited.

"Um, I think I need another lesson first so that—" you start to say.

"No way," Becca says, cutting you off. "You can practice here. And don't worry about falling—it's just part of snow-boarding."

 If you take another lesson, turn to page 103.

 If you follow Becca and Emmy, turn to page 119.

You grin and sing along with Shelby. The woods *are* like a winter wonderland. And you and Honey make a great team. But soon the snow falls harder. Icy flakes sting your cheeks as the wind whips the frigid air.

"Whoa!" Jen hollers from the front. "I need to check the map." You ski a little closer so that you can hear her better. "We're about a third of the way," Jen explains. "I think we should turn around here. It's getting hard to see."

You're disappointed, but then Jen asks you and Honey to lead the way back. "Dare needs a rest from breaking the trail," she says. "Are you and Honey up for it?"

"Yes!" you say without missing a beat. Following your tracks back to the school should be easy.

But soon you realize how difficult it is to be first. Snow clings to Honey's soft fur, and she's panting hard from plowing through the deepening drifts. Your goggles keep getting covered, so you can barely see. And the blowing wind has erased your original tracks.

What if you take the wrong trail? Your confidence falters as you imagine leading the club away from the school. Should you let someone more experienced lead?

 If you stop and ask someone else to go in front, turn to page 94.

 If you forge ahead in the lead, turn to page 96.

"Bye, Shelby!" you say, waving, as your heart flutters in your chest. Part of you wishes you were waiting for the chairlift with Shelby, but you don't want Becca to think you're a wimp. You already bailed on her yesterday.

You glide on your board over to Becca. A chill wind stings your cheeks, and you try not to glance down the plunging slope. "Let's stick together," you tell Becca. "For safety's sake."

"Good idea," says Becca, lowering her goggles. "Follow me!"

You lower your own goggles, tell yourself to quit worrying, and turn the nose of your board downhill. Shifting your weight to your back foot, you start off at an angle. There's no going back now.

You traverse the first section of Lightning Bolt at a steady pace, but then the trail splits. Becca veers toward the left. That trail is marked with a zigzag, which means difficult. The right-hand trail is marked with a curvy line, which means intermediate.

You and Becca agreed to stay together. But are you a strong enough snowboarder to handle the tough trail?

 If you follow Becca onto the difficult trail, turn to page 97.

 If you stick with the intermediate trail, turn to page 95.

Stopping, you ask your friends, "Will someone else go first? Honey and I aren't doing so great."

"I can't," Jen calls from the back of the group. "My goggle strap is broken, and I can barely see."

You pause. The thought of staying in the lead gives you more chills than the blustery wind.

"I'll trade goggles with you, Jen," you say quickly. She must hear the worry in your voice, because she agrees. She picks her way carefully along the trail until she reaches your side, and you exchange goggles.

A half hour later, with Jen and Dare in the lead, the group makes it safely back to the school. But as you unharness Honey, who still seems to have lots of energy, you wonder if you *could* have led the group through the snowstorm. You'd like to be a strong leader like Jen. *Will I get another chance someday?* you ask yourself. *I hope so!*

The End

You have a strong gut feeling that the intermediate trail is the best choice for you.

You wish you could tell Becca that you've decided to play it safe, but she's too far ahead. Pivoting the nose of your board, you head right. You pass a girl being assisted by the ski patrol, and watch others take some nasty spills. You traverse the slope cautiously—glad that Shelby and Emmy were good teachers.

By the time you get to the bottom of the hill, your legs are shaking and you can't feel your fingers and toes. You search for Becca, but you don't see her.

You're proud you chose the intermediate trail, which was challenging enough. But you're also worried that when Becca finds out you took the easier slope, she'll call you a chicken—or a *turtle* for taking so long.

You stoop to take your boots from your bindings. Then again you hunt for Becca among the skiers and boarders. You're starting to get worried. Since she's so much faster than you, she should be finished already, shouldn't she?

 Turn to page 102.

Stopping to give Honey a rest, you glance back at your friends. Amber is bent over, checking Pepper's paw. "It's split," she tells you. "I'll need to put on a bootie."

Jen is messing with her googles. "The strap broke," she says, tossing the useless goggles into her pack. "It's good you're leading now."

"That's for sure!" Shelby exclaims, her voice muffled. Her scarf is wrapped around her chin so many times that you can barely see her face. "There's no way Chocolate Chip and I want to be in front," she says.

Looks as if it's up to you and Honey. You give her a pat. She woofs and pulls you forward, obviously eager to keep going. "Let's go!" you tell her when the others are ready.

As you ski along the trail, drifts cover your tracks. When the trail forks, you have no clue which is the right way.

Honey doesn't hesitate, though. She lopes toward the left. You have to trust her, you realize.

Suddenly, you see a light shining through the snow. It's the school. Honey found her way back!

As soon as you get to shelter, all the girls give you and Honey hugs. "Playing follow the leader was a no-brainer with you and Honey in front," Amber says.

You're proud of yourself—and of Honey. You were strong enough to take over the lead, and you trusted Honey to steer you in the right direction.

The End

You promised Becca you would stick with her, but a shiver of fear tingles up your arms. Several skiers and snowboarders zoom past, shredding down the difficult trail. By the smooth way they maneuver, you know they are way more skilled than you. Plus your legs are getting tired and your fingers are numb. But you proved you are good at traversing, so you decide you can handle the steep slope if you just keep it slow.

As soon as you start off, you realize that traversing isn't going to work. The slope is icy and bumpy, and edging is difficult. Your legs begin to shake with fatigue, and you wish you were safe at the bottom.

Even worse, there's no sign of Becca ahead of you. Where is your friend?

Turn to page 100.

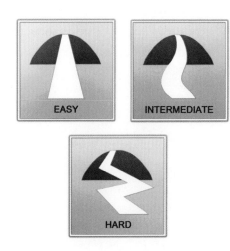

"Don't look so discouraged," Amber says. You must have been looking as droopy as Honey for her to notice.

"Sorry, Amber. I guess I thought this would be easier," you say, shrugging. "I thought Honey would love dog-sledding as much as Pepper. Or maybe I'm just not good at training dogs."

"Hey, you're doing great!" Amber says. "You've been super patient with Honey. Pepper is a husky, so he's been bred to pull. And remember, there's strength in numbers. It takes a team of dogs working together to pull a sled smoothly—just like it might take a team of girls plus one husky to get Honey moving!" she adds with a laugh.

You can't help but grin. Amber's encouragement boosts your spirits, and it turns out that she's right about teamwork. To get Honey—and the sled—moving, you run ahead holding a cheese treat while Amber rides on the sled.

"Come on, Honey!" you call as Amber gives Pepper the "let's go" command. Pepper bounds forward, tugging Honey with him, and soon the four of you are trotting in the snow around the school.

Turn to page 101.

Suddenly, you hit a patch of ice, and your board scoots out from under you. Arms flailing, you fall backward onto the packed snow.

As you push yourself up, you see a red helmet and an arm waving from beneath the trees that border the slope. *Becca!* She's sitting down, her left boot unstrapped from her board.

"I'm fine," she calls when you reach her side, "but my right binding is loose. I took a pretty big fall."

You pull your mini tool kit from your pocket. "Lucky for you, Shelby believes in being prepared," you tell Becca. Even though your fingers are numb, you manage to tighten the screws so that Becca's binding is secure on her board.

"Thanks," Becca says. "Sorry I pressured you into going this way," she adds as she stares down the trail.

You shrug. "I could have said no," you admit. "But we're not far from the intermediate trail. Should we walk uphill and take that one instead?"

You're relieved when Becca agrees with you.

You unstrap one boot from your board and make your way up the slope, stepping with one foot and sliding the board with the other. When you reach the sign, you strap your boot to the board and follow Becca downhill.

As you traverse downward, you realize that Shelby wasn't just smart about the tool kit. She also made the right decision about Lightning Bolt. Next time, *you'll* be strong enough to know your limits, too.

The End

When you glance backward over your shoulder, you see a change in Honey. Her ears are pricked and her eyes glowing. She's enjoying this!

Stopping, you step off the trail and let the sled fly by. "Haw!" Amber shouts. At first Honey obeys because she's beside Pepper, but soon they're working as a team. Amber circles the sled around. "Whoa!" The dogs halt in front of you. Honey's panting happily.

"She loves it!" you exclaim to Amber. Stooping on one knee, you give Honey a hug.

"I thought she would once she got started," Amber says, her eyes glowing, too. She steps off the runners. "Your turn!"

Instantly, worry makes your insides tighten. Just because Honey and Pepper mushed for Amber doesn't mean the two will listen to you. But you can't give up now. Amber and Pepper have worked too hard helping you. Plus, you've been waiting for this day—when you finally find out if all the training and patience will pay off.

🌟 Turn to page 107.

Just then, you spy Becca gliding down the slope toward you. Her cheeks are pale, and she's moving stiffly. "I hit a rough patch of ice," she blurts. "I tumbled down the slope for *forever* before I could stop. I've never been so scared!"

You're shocked. You thought Becca was fearless! You help her with her board and lead her to the chalet, where Shelby is waiting with hot chocolate. As you sip your hot chocolate, you toast your friends. "Here's to Shelby, a great teacher," you say. "And to Becca, a great snowboarder who handled a tough spill."

"And was strong enough to admit she was afraid," adds Shelby.

"Here's to *you* for trying something new!" says Becca.

You grin as you take a sip from your mug. The chocolate is good, but the compliment from Becca is even *sweeter*.

The End

A strong girl admits when she's afraid.

INNERSTAR UNIVERSITY

"Thanks, Becca, for thinking that I'm ready for tricks," you say. "But I'm not."

Becca scowls for a second. Then she points a finger at you and says, "Fine, but after your lesson, come find us at the park. Got it?" You nod, but you wish she wouldn't be so pushy.

You sign up for a beginner lesson, since yesterday you skipped some of the basics. The instructor shows you how to traverse, slideslip, and fall without hurting yourself. On the bunny slope, you even try a teensy ollie, shifting your weight onto your back foot and using the tail of the board like a spring to "pop" you off the snow a few inches.

After the lesson, you head to the snowboarding park. Becca and Emma are jumping over a small "table top." It's not for you, but you see a perfect place to practice your ollies. Over and over you spring into the air, straighten your board, and land with bent knees. When you try an ollie going faster, you lift even higher off the ground and catch some air. The rush is thrilling, and you hear clapping. Becca and Emmy are cheering from the sidelines.

You smile with pride. You're glad that you tried snowboarding. It's super fun! You're also glad that you were strong enough to follow your own path. Next time, maybe you'll be ready to challenge Becca and Emmy with even *bigger* tricks.

The End

Saturday morning, you rent cross-country skis, which are longer than downhill skis. Paige shows you how to sync up your push, glide, arm, and pole movements, and soon you're gliding along a short cross-country trail. It's fun!

Paige stops on a snow-covered peak and looks down onto campus, nestled in the valley where there is no snow. She points out a hawk soaring along the cliff beneath you.

Later, you're the one who spots hare tracks heading off the ski trail into the woods. "Paige, here's your chance for your picture!" you say. "Let's follow them."

"Not so fast," Paige says. "We should stay on the trail."

 If you push Paige to head into the woods and follow the hare, turn to page 109.

If you stay on the trail, turn to page 106.

Yesterday, you were flying down Falling Star. You can't believe Paige thinks going off the trail is daring.

"Sorry," says Paige as she starts gliding again ahead of you. "Staying on the trail is one of Sky-High's rules—and mine."

Your shoulders slump. Paige is right: staying on the trail is safe. *Too* safe. For a moment, you wish you were zipping over the whale tail in the snowboard park with Becca.

Sighing, you turn and head down the trail, hoping that the shy hare might hop out in front of you so that you have something exciting to tell Becca and Emma later. But the only thing you meet on the winding snow-covered path is someone from ski patrol.

Ahead of you, Paige is silent. *Maybe she's sad that she didn't get a shot of that hare,* you think. Instead she finally turns around and says, "I bet this is boring for you. Would you rather be snowboarding with Becca?"

Uh-oh. Can she read your mind?

 Turn to page 108.

Grasping the handlebars, you climb onto the sled, one foot on each runner. You take a deep breath, give Amber a thumbs-up, and then call, "Let's go!"

Honey turns and looks quizzically at you, as if trying to figure out why you're behind him instead of in front with treats. But when Pepper bounds off, Honey is forced to follow. The sled starts gliding. You circle around the school, where some of the other girls are mushing their own teams.

As you give commands, you notice Pepper doesn't respond as well to your voice—he's used to Amber, after all. But the two dogs are working well enough for you to follow another sled down a trail.

The dogs lope through the snow almost silently as you glide along behind. The sun sparkles through the branches overhead, warming your face, and you take a moment to breathe it all in.

At a fork in the trail, you call "gee" to turn right and circle back to the school. The other team is going left, but you don't want to keep Amber waiting. Pepper, however, keeps heading left.

You shift your weight. "Gee!" you call again. Ignoring you, Pepper makes a sharp left, his ears pricked, his attention on something in the woods. Suddenly two deer burst from the trees and bound down the trail, Pepper hot on their heels.

🐾 Turn to page 118.

"No! I'm enjoying this," you say quickly. "It's nice out here." It's the truth—the woods are peaceful and beautiful, something you don't have time to notice when you're skiing or snowboarding. "It's just that Becca is so enthusiastic about snowboarding," you add.

Paige giggles. "Yeah, it's hard to say no to her sometimes," she says.

You're surprised to hear Paige say that. "But *you* aren't afraid to ignore Becca and do your own thing," you tell her. "I wish I were more like you."

Suddenly, behind Paige, you spy a red spot against the white snow. It's a fox!

"Paige, get your camera ready and turn around slowly," you whisper. She does, raises her camera, and snaps several shots. The fox shoots you a curious look and then disappears into the brush.

Your heart is pounding just as hard as if you were zipping over the whale tail. There's no place you'd rather be right now than standing on this trail with Paige, a strong girl who knows what she loves to do. From now on, *you'll* practice being strong, too. Following your heart—and a quiet trail—can lead to happy surprises!

The End

"Come on, Paige, don't you want to follow that hare and have an adventure?" you ask.

Paige finally says, "Okay, but let's not go too far."

"Yay! Get your camera ready," you say as you set off into the woods. There's no groomed trail, but the snow is easy to glide through as you follow the hare's tracks. It begins to snow, and you feel as if you and Paige are true nature girls. It's so quiet in the woods that you can almost hear the snowflakes falling.

But, wow, that hare is sure elusive—and quick. The tracks dart right and left, under branches, around tall tree trunks, and through brush.

"We're too far off the trail. We need to turn back," Paige calls from behind you.

Stopping, you realize that you were so intent on finding the hare that you didn't notice how hard it was snowing. Now the tracks you're following are being covered by the falling snow.

 Turn to page 114.

"I'm sorry, Honey," you say, hugging the pup. "I'm kind of a coward, too, but it wasn't right to take it out on you."

Honey gives you a sweet slurp. Now that all's forgiven, you try a new approach. "Hey, look at how much fun Pepper is having in the snow!" you say, pointing. Honey pricks her ears. Leaping over your legs, she dashes toward Pepper. Soon the two dogs are chasing each other around.

After playtime, the lesson begins. Jen supervises while you and Amber harness and hook up the two dogs, side by side. Amber takes them for a run first. She's a confident musher, and Honey looks right at home. She bounds along beside Pepper, the ribbons on her harness waving in the air.

When it's your turn, you practice simple commands as you mush in a loop around the school. All your practice has made you more confident, too. But when you call "haw" for the dogs to turn left, Honey veers right, yanking Pepper.

"Honey, haw," you say firmly, but she sits in the snow and doesn't move.

You almost lose your patience again, but you don't. Up to now, Honey's done so well. Could something be wrong?

You set your *snow hook* just as Jen showed you, by kicking the metal hook into the snow to keep the sled in place. Then you check the lines, but they're not tangled. When you lift up Honey's paw, you see the problem. Honey has snowballs packed in her paws. They look painful. Poor girl!

Turn to page 116.

"Whoa!" you call to Pepper, hoping you can get both dogs to stop so that you can find the right trail. But Pepper is running so intently that he ignores your command.

Up ahead, the trail forks again. A snowmobile sign marks the left-hand trail. The dogsledding sign is on the right. You can't make a mistake this time.

"Gee!" you tell Pepper. He's running so hard, it's as if he doesn't hear. But before you can call "gee" again, Honey swings right, forcing Pepper to follow.

You smile, excited that Honey was the one to obey. But you're not out of the woods yet. This trail is taking you up the mountain away from the school. You can tell Pepper and Honey are tiring, and your arms and legs are shaking.

You need to find the trail back to the school—soon!

Turn to page 115.

"You're right, Paige," you admit as you quickly turn around. "We can follow our ski tracks back to the trail."

Gliding and swinging, the two of you make good time following your zigzagging tracks backward. Then you ski through some brush and totally lose the trail.

"Paige," you call over your shoulder, "the snow covered our ski marks!" Your stomach flip-flops. Without a trail to follow, you'll never find your way out of the woods.

Paige skis up close behind you and peers over your shoulder.

"I'm sorry," you apologize to your friend. "It's my fault we're lost. I shouldn't have pushed you to do something you didn't want to do." *Isn't that what Becca did to me yesterday?* you think.

"Lost?" Paige laughs. "Don't worry. I always know where I am." She whips out a GPS, explaining, "I hike so much, I'm always prepared. I have a cell phone, too, to call ski patrol."

You giggle with relief. A GPS and a cell phone? So much for being nature girls! "Thanks for being prepared," you tell Paige. "And thanks for not blaming me. Next time, I'll be a better partner and follow your lead—instead of leading us both off track!"

The End

"Whoa," you call, and both dogs slow and then halt. "Good boy—and girl."

Getting off the sled, you set your *snow hook*, a large metal hook that you kick into the snow to hold the sled in place. You take a moment to pat both dogs' heads, and then you open up the map Jen gave you. You stare at the zigzag of lines—some blue, some red, and others green. Green for "go"?

You frown worriedly. You have no idea how to read the map or where you are. There's a square where the school is located, but there's no convenient X to mark the spot where you are now, so you have no clue which squiggly line to take. Oh, why didn't you pay more attention to Jen's instructions on map reading before rushing off?

Think, you tell yourself. *Calm down and think.* Should you turn around and follow your own tracks back? No, that seems dangerous—you might come face-to-face with the snowmobile. And who knows? The snowmobile might have already erased your tracks.

You glance down at Honey and Pepper. They're staring at up at you, waiting for you to make a decision. Stooping, you give them each a hug. "I'm sorry," you say, trying not to cry. "It's my fault that we're lost!"

Turn to page 117.

You know just the thing to help Honey. Booties!

Amber knows where to find them. She hurries into the school's office and comes out with a cute set of booties, which look like socks—with bows. Amber shows you how to fit them over Honey's paws and secure them.

Off you go again! At first, Honey lifts her paws in the air awkwardly. But soon she gets used to the booties. Pepper leads the way, guiding you and Honey skillfully along the trail. Beside Pepper, Honey gives her all, but you have to laugh at the bows on her harness and her booties.

As you head through the woods, sparkling with snow, you remember back to your first "run" with Honey on campus. You worried whether you were strong enough to lead. Now you know you are. You've become a trainer with many strengths, and *patience* tops them all.

The End

"Hello!" a cheery voice calls out. Startled, you glance up. Paige is skiing toward you on cross-country skis.

"Paige!" you cry, jumping up to give her a huge hug. "What are you doing on the dogsledding trail?"

She points behind her. "The ski trail crosses the dog trail a few yards back," she explains. "I saw you go by. You looked a little, um . . ."

"Lost?" you say, flushing. "Amber gave me a map, but I didn't really look at it, and then I gave Pepper the wrong command." Your shoulders slump.

"Don't worry, you're not far from the school," Paige says, showing you on your map. "The dogsled trail is red," she says, tracing it with her finger. "Go left when the trail forks up ahead, and it will circle back to the school."

You give Paige a hearty thank-you and follow her in the sled for a few yards until she turns right onto the ski trail. "Thanks again!" you call, waving until she disappears on the snowy path.

"Let's go," you tell Pepper and Honey. The dogs must sense they're headed home, because they pick up speed quickly.

As you glide through the woods, you try to muster the strength to admit to Jen and Amber that your impatience got you lost. Fortunately, Paige was there for you. Next time, you'll lean on Amber, too, because now you know that friends are stronger *together*.

The End

The sled tips. "Whoa!" you call as you wobble on the runners. Pepper speeds ahead, but Honey obeys your command. She slows to a trot, making Pepper slow down, too.

"Good girl, Honey!" you praise after catching your breath. Braking, you find an open spot along the trail to turn the sled around. As you mush back toward the school, you realize that this time, *Honey* is leading Pepper.

When you see Amber waiting by the school, you wave excitedly. "We did it!" you say. "Thanks for your help, Amber. We made a great team."

"See?" she says. "There's strength in numbers."

Amber is right. You couldn't have trained Honey by yourself. But today on the trail, Honey proved her strength as a sled dog, and you proved *yours* as her trainer.

The End

There's strength in numbers.

INNERSTAR UNIVERSITY

"Okay," you say, giving in to Becca, who is already hurrying off toward the whale tail.

As you nervously strap your boots onto the board, you watch several kids ride the snow-covered hump. Becca's right—most of them take a tumble. *Ouch*, you think.

"Don't worry," Emmy says. "We'll start on something smaller." She points to a low ramp that several pint-sized kids are gliding down.

As you watch Emmy ride down the ramp, your heart does little leaps. Then it's your turn. Pointing the nose of your board toward the ramp, you glide down the hill. You zip off the ramp—too fast! Your arms windmill and your legs stiffen. When you land, your board scoots out from beneath you. You sail down the hill on your back.

"Watch o-u-t!" you holler. *Thump!* You hit something hard, which stops your slide. Becca!

Her face is as red as her helmet—from laughing. "That was radical!" she says. "Good thing you ran into me, though. You could have wiped out some kid."

"I'm *not* ready for the park," you tell Becca as you wipe the snow from your face. "I need to head back to the bunny hill." You should have told her this earlier. You're not hurt, but you could have been—or you could have hurt someone else, even Becca. Next time, you need to be strong enough to resist her and make the best decision for *you*.

The End

Glossary of Sled-Dog Commands:

Let's go: Get moving!

Gee: Go right

Haw: Go left

On by: Pass another team or other distraction

Easy: Slow down

Whoa: Stop